TEETH

Written by Alan Durant

Collins

CHAPTER 1

One gloomy, breezy afternoon in autumn, Carl and his younger brother, Joe, were on the beach by the old pier. They often went there to meet with friends or just to throw stones into the sea. Sometimes they'd tell each other spooky stories. The old pier with its rotten, creaky planks was a good setting for telling and listening to spooky stories. They liked trying to scare each other – and they liked being a bit scared too.

Carl ducked behind one of the pier's chunky old pillars. "I'm the ghost of the pier and I'm coming to get you," he whispered into the wind.

Joe laughed. "Well I'm a ghost buster and I'm not scared of you."

He bent down to pick up some seaweed to throw at Carl and felt something sharp in the sand.

"Hey, what's this?" he said. He dug in the sand with his hand. Carl came over to join him.

"It's some teeth," said Joe. "I wonder what they came from."

Joe held the teeth out in his palm. They were big – about the size of his little finger – and caramel coloured. Thin black lines like cracks ran through them. They were shaped like the letter "Y" and were very sharp too. Joe pricked his finger with one of them and it drew blood. "Ow, that's sharp!" he yelped.

Carl laughed. "Don't be a baby," he said. He took the teeth from Joe. "I reckon they're shark's teeth," he said. "Or maybe they're vampire teeth," he grinned, holding the teeth up at each side of his mouth.

"They're really big," said Joe. His eyes widened with excitement. "They might be dinosaur teeth!"

"What would a dinosaur be doing on a beach?" scoffed Carl. "They are good, though, whatever they came from."

The brothers decided that they would have one tooth each. They took the teeth home, thinking about how they would impress their friends. Joe put his tooth on the shelf above his desk next to some stones and shells and a dried-up starfish — his other treasures from the sea. He liked the way it looked there and decided it was the best of all his treasures.

Carl tied some thin string round his tooth and wore it around his neck. He liked to imagine that it had magical powers. He imagined he was a superhero – Tigerman or Sharkman, hero of the sea! Dangling from his neck, the tooth appeared to Carl to gleam. There was a tiny spot of red from where Joe's finger had bled on it.

That was cool, Carl thought.

CHAPTER 2

That night a storm blew up. The wind rattled on Carl's window.
He woke up. It took a few moments for his eyes to get used to
the gloom. His room wasn't totally dark because his bedroom
door was open and the landing light was on. His curtains
weren't drawn, because he liked them that way so that he
could see the night outside. Slowly, he looked over. What was
that at the window? He thought he saw a dark shape outside.
Was that a paw pressing against the pane, a giant paw?
He was sure he could hear angry breathing too – or was it
just the wind?

Carl got out of bed and went over to the window ... but there
was nothing there. He pulled the curtains tight across
the window and got back into bed. Suddenly, the curtains
billowed away from the window into the room as if blown by
a strong breeze. But the window was shut ...
Carl shivered and turned his face
to the wall.

In the bedroom next door, Joe woke up too. Something with very sharp claws was scratching at his window, trying to get in. No, it was just a branch of a tree scraping against the glass – wasn't it? Of course it was, he told himself. There was nothing out there. And yet ... Just for an instant he thought he felt something sharp against his skin.

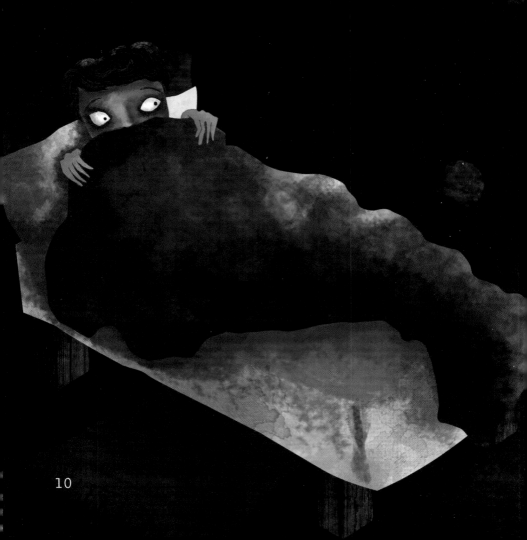

The room suddenly turned icy cold. Joe pulled the duvet over his head, but he couldn't get warm. He lay awake for ages shaking, with a hard ball of fear in the pit of his stomach.

The next morning the brothers talked about their dreams.
Usually they would have laughed at each other and said,
"That was a good one." But this morning was different.
It wasn't a joke. Joe was really scared.

"What if those teeth really did belong to a vampire?" he said.
"Or a flesh-eating beast?"

"There's no such thing as vampires," said Carl lightly.
"It was just your imagination." He said this to try to make
Joe feel better, but actually he'd been spooked too.

12

They thought about what to do. "Let's take the teeth to
the museum in town," said Carl at last. "Old Mac will know
what creature they came from." Old Mac, Mr Macdonald,
owned the museum.

"Good idea," Joe agreed, perking up a little. "Hey, perhaps
they'll be valuable and we'll get a reward."

"Yeah," said Carl. They thought about what they would
do with the reward and started to forget about their fears.

After school, Joe and Carl took the teeth to the museum.
They often went there. They loved the many skulls and
skeletons and stuffed wild animals on display. The museum
was gloomy and dusty and, like the old pier, had an air of
dark mystery about it.

Old Mac was at his desk. He seemed to be asleep. With his
wild grey hair and old-fashioned clothes, he fitted in well
with the museum's exhibits.

Carl coughed loudly and Old Mac's eyes sprang open.

"Eh? What?" he muttered.

"It's only us," laughed Carl.

"Well, what do you want?" Old Mac grumped.

The brothers showed him the teeth.

"Can you tell us what creature they come from?" Joe asked.

Old Mac frowned. "Do you think I've got nothing better to do with my time?" he grumbled. "I've got exhibits to sort, you know."

Joe and Carl smiled at one another. The exhibits in the museum had never changed since the first day they'd come in, years before. Hardly anyone visited the place. Joe and Carl were by far the museum's best customers. They were used to Old Mac's ways. He could be grumpy sometimes, but he was full of interesting information. He was actually quite friendly too when you got to know him.

Old Mac peered at the teeth through his glasses.
Then he sighed. "Follow me," he said and he led the boys
into a back room. The brothers grinned at each other.
This place was full of old stuff. There were boxes and cases
from floor to ceiling. Peeping out from among them was
the skeleton of some sort of animal. On a table in a glass
display case, a wild bird of prey glared out, claws raised as
if about to attack.

Joe looked at the claws and thought about the scratching he'd heard at his window the night before. "Maybe it was just a bird I heard last night," Joe whispered. Carl nodded.

Old Mac put the teeth under a microscope. Then he focused it carefully to examine them. In the gloomy room, the teeth seemed to glow. Joe and Carl waited impatiently. They were sure those teeth were special. But what did they come from?

Old Mac stood up straight. He shuffled over to a shelf and took down a thick, tatty old book. He put it on the counter. Dust puffed into the air.

"Now, boys, what do you think these teeth belong to?" he asked.

"A shark?" said Carl.

"A dinosaur?" said Joe.

The museum owner shook his head. "They do come from a creature," he said gravely, "but neither of those."

He opened the book and pointed at a picture on the page.
"That's what they come from," he declared. The brothers
stared at the picture eagerly. Then their faces creased
in disgust.

"A dog!" they cried.

"I'm afraid so," said Old Mac, chuckling. "They come from
a dog – a big dog."

"I can't believe it," said Carl, and Joe shook his head with
disappointment.

CHAPTER 3

It was dark when the brothers made their way home. Crisp brown leaves rustled about their feet in the breeze.

"A dog," sighed Carl.

"Well, at least it wasn't anything scary," said Joe.

"No," Carl agreed. "I'm not scared of a dog."

At that moment there was a noise behind them. It sounded like a growl. The boys turned.

Was there something moving in the darkness?

Carl laughed. "We're a pair of scaredy cats, aren't we?" he said.

Joe laughed too, but a little nervously. He wanted to get home quickly, out of the dark. "Let's take the shortcut home across the beach," he suggested. Carl agreed.

When they got to the beach, the wind was blowing waves of sand towards the sea to meet the waves of water that were lapping into the shore. Out at sea, a single fishing boat slipped across the bay. The only sounds were the rumble and hiss of the waves and, now and then, a whoosh as they slapped against the old pier. The brothers walked quickly across the sand.

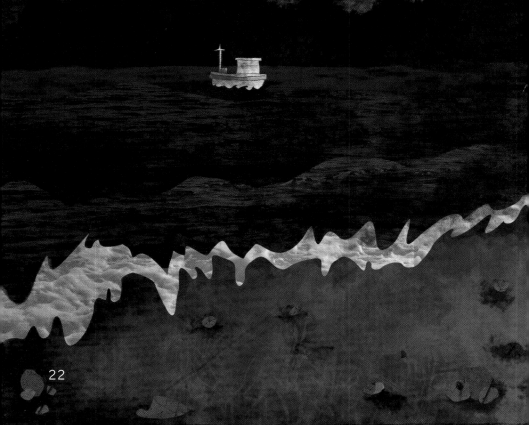

"Old Mac had a good laugh at us there, didn't he?" said Carl.

"I reckon that's the most he's laughed for years," Joe added.

Suddenly, a blood-curdling howl pierced the darkness. The boys stopped in their tracks. They thought they could hear panting and the soft patter of paws on the sand. They turned, but they couldn't see anything, so they started to walk faster. Then the panting and pattering started up again. It was getting closer ... and closer.

"Something's following us," gasped Carl with a shiver.

Joe was too scared to say anything. He had goose bumps all over. The boys started to run, their feet slipping on the sand and pebbles, but the panting and pattering kept on coming closer. There was another bloodcurdling howl — right behind them this time ...

They turned once more and in the bright moonlight they saw
... an enormous hound! It was as big as a lion, and there was
a ghostly gleam around it. It growled fiercely and bared its
massive, fearsome teeth. Blood dripped from its huge jaws.
It stood up on its hind legs with its paws raised. Its claws
were as sharp as spears. Its eyes were fiery red, wild,
terrifying. It was not like any dog the boys had ever seen.
This was a creature of nightmares, of horror.

"Look!" Carl breathed.

The ghostly dog had two teeth missing.

"I th-think it wants its t-teeth," stammered Joe.

"We'd better give them back or he'll tear us to pieces," Carl whispered.

The hound snarled and raised its claws higher. The boys shuddered. Then they dropped the teeth in the sand by the old pier, just where they had found them, turned and ran for their lives. They ran and ran, racing through the dark, never once daring to look back, until, breathless and scared, they arrived home.

From that night on, Carl and Joe never picked up anything on the beach, not even a pebble. And they never ever went back to the old pier again.

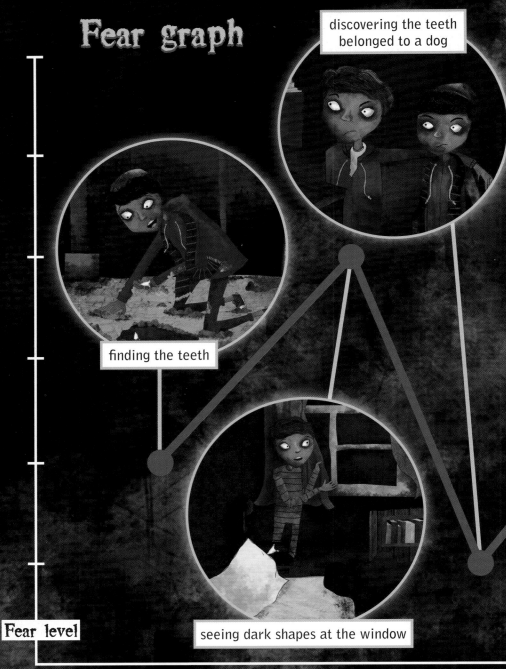

Fear graph

discovering the teeth belonged to a dog

finding the teeth

seeing dark shapes at the window

Fear level

hearing the blood curdling howl

seeing the hound

walking through the woods, hearing strange noises

Ideas for reading

Written by Gillian Howell
Primary Literacy Consultant

Reading objectives:
- predict what might happen on the basis of what has been read so far
- make inferences on the basis of what is being said and done
- discuss the sequence of events in books and how items of information are related

Spoken language objectives:
- use spoken language to develop understanding through speculating, imagining and exploring ideas
- give well-structured descriptions, explanations and narratives for different purposes, including for expressing feelings
- articulate and justify answers, arguments and opinions
- maintain attention and participate actively in collaborative conversations

Curriculum links: History

Interest words: souvenirs, autumn, pier, palm, dinosaur, treasures, curtains, stomach, imagination, museum, creature, valuable, exhibits, ceiling, microscope, impatiently, special, fiercely

Word count: 1,874

Resources: pens, paper

Build a context for reading

- Look at the cover and read the title. Ask the children to predict the setting of the story from the cover artwork.

- Read the back cover blurb. Ask the children to say what sort of story they think this will be, e.g. funny, scary or exciting?

- Explain that this is a mystery story. Ask the children to predict what the mystery will be from the title and cover illustration.

Understand and apply reading strategies

- Ask the children to read the story together. Remind them to use their phonic knowledge and contextual clues to work out new words.

- As they read, pause at significant events, e.g. on pp8–9, ask the children to discuss the storm. What effect does it have on the mood of the story?

- Ask the children to read to the end of the book. Praise them for reading with expression and support children who need extra help.